Arty!

The First Artist in Space

williambee

PAVILION

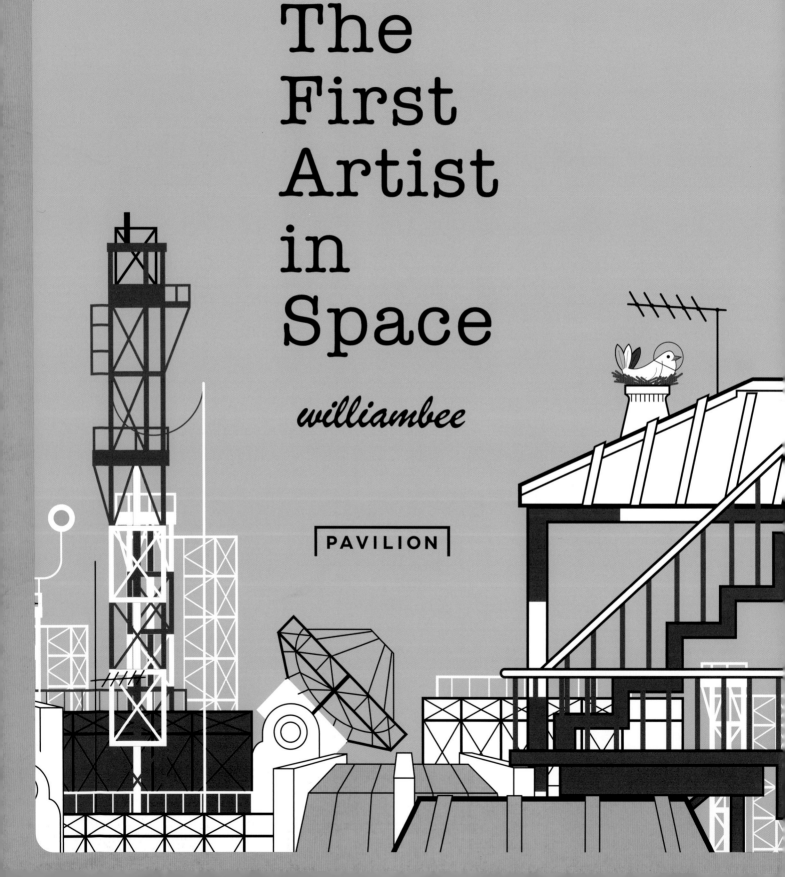

Space!

Who's been there?

People, monkeys, dogs, cats, rabbits, guinea pigs, mice, tortoises, flies, worms, spiders, beetles, shrimps, moths and... fungi!

And who hasn't been there?

Artists!

Because every year the scientists at the space laboratories have asked a famous artist to go up into space – to paint it.

And every year the famous artists have said...

Until one day
the scientists visited Paris
to ask if Arty would like to be
the first artist in space.

And Mr Grimaldi
(who sells Arty's paintings)
said...

"YES!!!!!"

Arty arrives at the space laboratories, ready for his painting holiday in space.

The scientists are delighted to see him.

So delighted they straight away put him through some rigorous space tests.

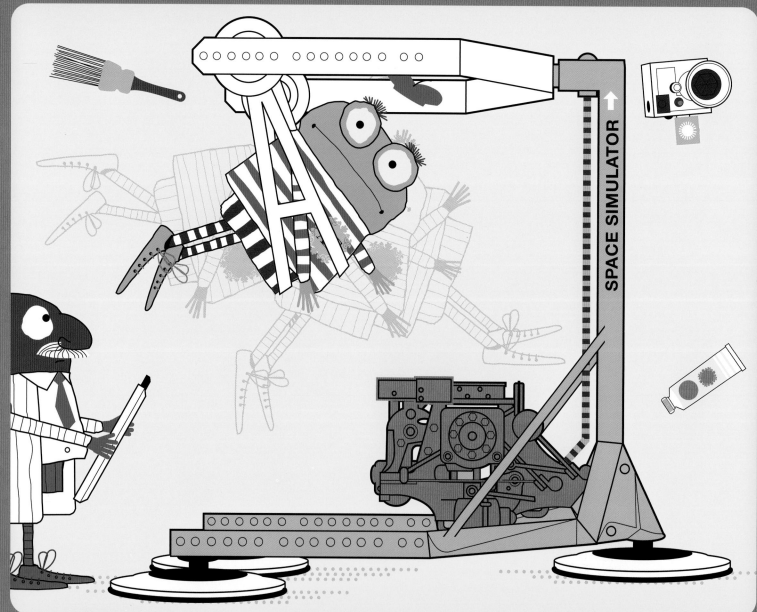

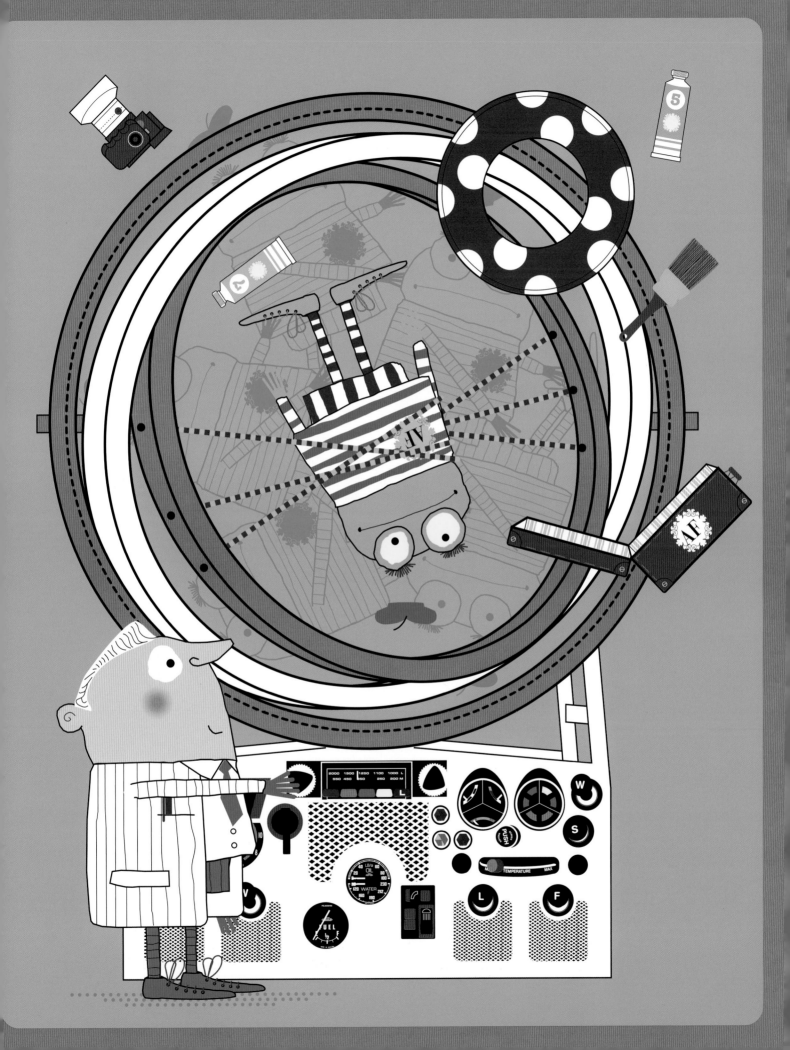

Arty passes all the tests...
...well, about as well as the fungi did, anyway.

And
afterwards
he has
a little
lie down.

Then Arty is measured and fitted
with his special Artist's Space Suit.

And they do it all over again...

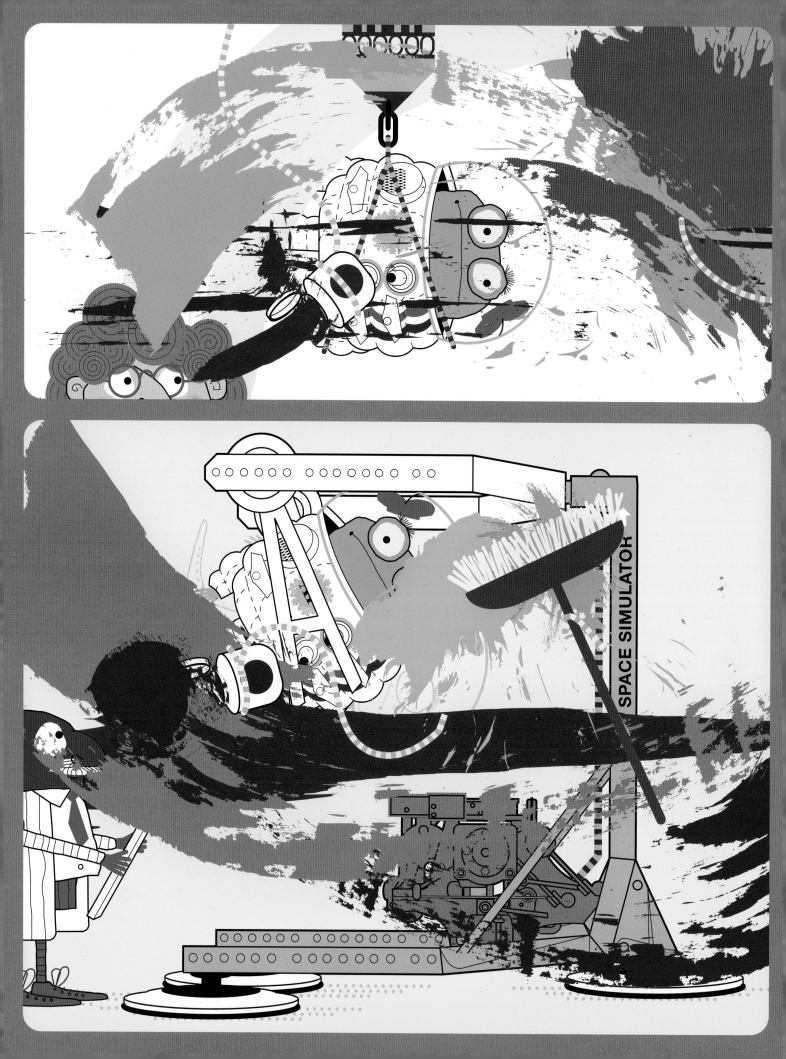

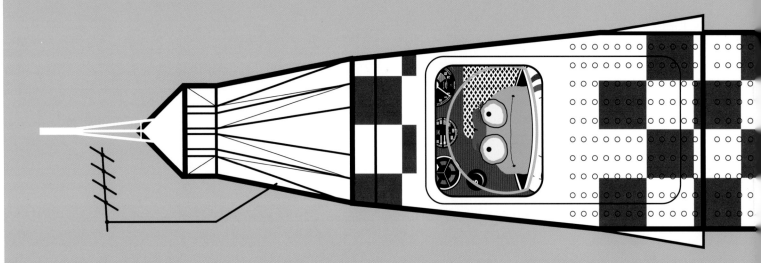

And after Arty
– and all the
scientists –
have had another
little lie down...

...up he goes!

Arty lands... somewhere.
"What a dump!" he says.
"There's nothing to paint here."

The space scientists will be
very angry!

But then Arty has an idea –
and rushes to get all his paints,
brushes, brooms and buckets.

Arty mostly uses his favourite colours
- green and yellow.

He races about: so little time
- so much to paint.

A
happy
Arty
heads
home.

The
space
scientists
should
be
happy
too!

But the space scientists
aren't happy at all!

"Where are the space paintings?"
they ask.

Arty points at the giant telescope.

"Have a look through that thing. You're in for a BIG surprise!" he says.

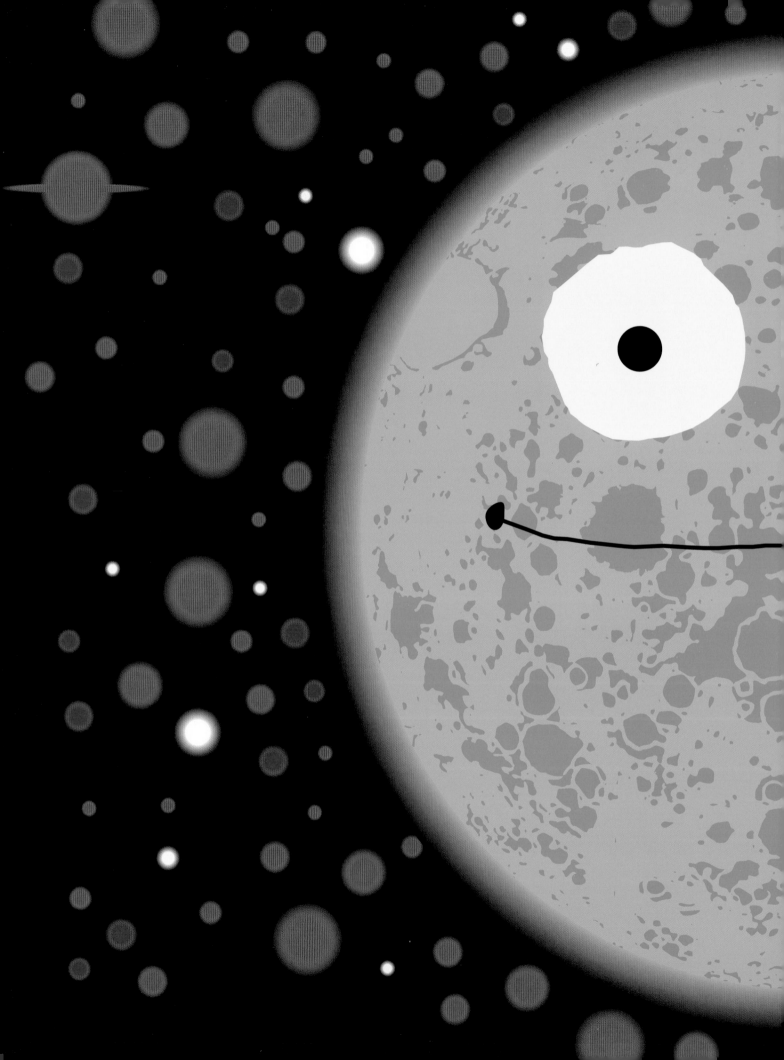

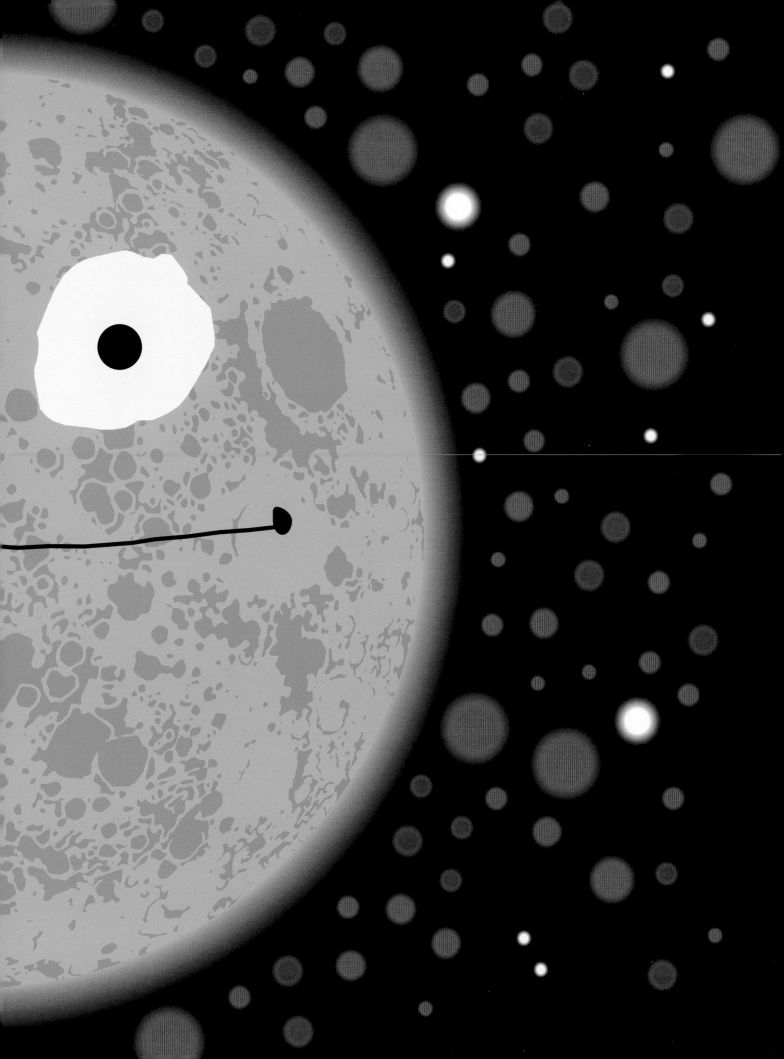

It IS a BIG surprise – and the space scientists don't like it AT ALL.

But Mr Grimaldi (who sells Arty's paintings) LOVES it! "I can sell it for MILLIONS!" he grins.